On her way out she met Bobby,
the boy next door.
"What a jolly brolly,"
said Bobby.

"This is no ordinary brolly," said Molly.

"My brolly and I have…

"...zoomed to the moon,
where we saw a rocket ship
and we searched for little
green moon men."

Molly walked to the park to see the ducks.
"What a jolly brolly," said the park keeper.
"This is no ordinary brolly," said Molly.

"My brolly and I have...

"...sailed the seas,
where we met some pirates
and had tea and cake
on their ship."

Molly and her brolly sat down
next to a little old lady.
"What a jolly brolly,"
said the old lady.

"This is no ordinary brolly," said Molly.
"My brolly and I have…

"...flown through
the clouds
to a magic castle,
deep in the woods
where I was princess for a day."

Molly went to see Mr Green
in the Sweetie Shop.
"What a jolly brolly," said Mr Green.

"This is no ordinary brolly," said Molly.

"My brolly and I have…

"…sailed down the cherryade river
to the land of sweets, where
the hills are made of jelly
and I munched and chewed
'til my tummy was full."

When Molly and her brolly
got home, Mum asked,
"Where have you been?"

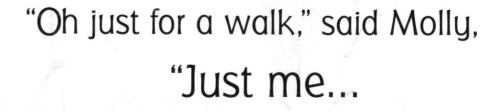

"Oh just for a walk," said Molly,
"Just me...

"...and my brolly!"

For Mum and Dad,
With all my love
E.J.W.

First published in 2006
by Meadowside Children's Books
185 Fleet Street
London EC4A 2HS

Text and Illustrations © Erica-Jane Waters
The right of Erica-Jane Waters to be identified
as the author and illustrator has been asserted
by her in accordance with the Copyright,
Designs and Patents Act, 1988

A CIP catalogue record for this book
is available from the British Library

ISBN 10 pbk 1-84539-188-8
ISBN 13 pbk 978-1-84539-188-1
ISBN 10 hbk 1-84539-189-6
ISBN 13 hbk 978-1-84539-189-8

10 9 8 7 6 5 4 3 2 1
Printed in China